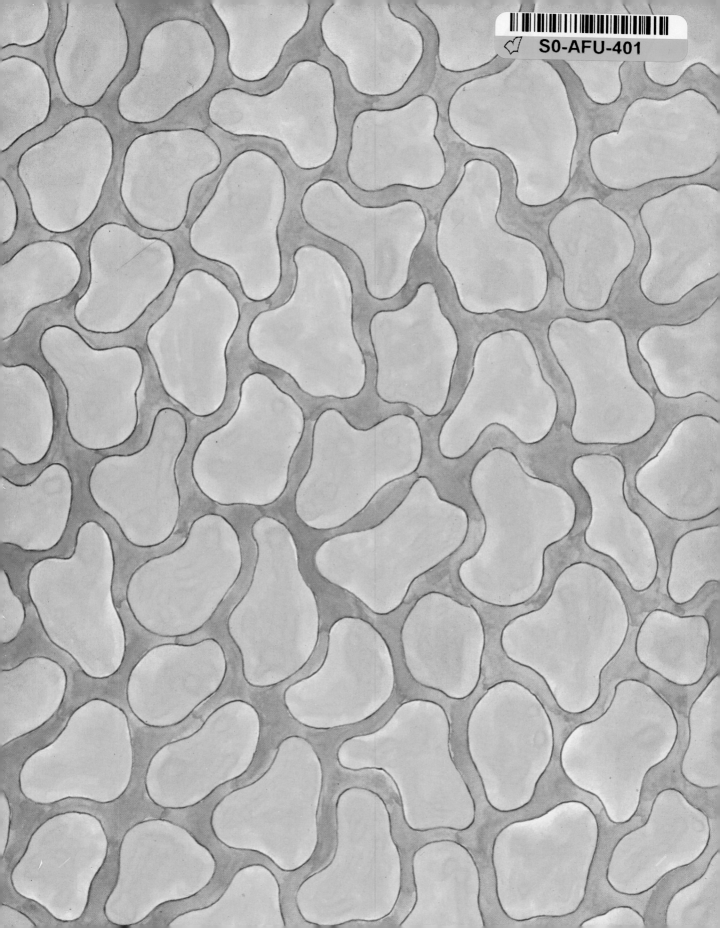

Parakeets and Peach Pies

BY KAY SMITH   PICTURES BY JOSE ARUEGO

PARENTS' MAGAZINE PRESS
NEW YORK

For Tommie Barkdull
(because this could almost happen at your house)

When Matthew came home from school, he saw his mother sitting on the porch steps.
"Mom! Mom!" he called, running up the path.
"I have to ask you something right away!"
"Just a minute," Mother said. "I want to show you something first."
Matthew followed his mother into the house.

"Hey!" he cried. "The hall's a mess!"
The dining room was worse.

And after one look at the living room, Matthew gasped,
"What happened to our house?"
Mother sat down on the sofa and gave a big sigh.
"Well," she said, "today the Ladies Literary League
met here for lunch and...

"your parakeet perched on Mrs. Parker's piece of peach pie and pecked at the pastry.

"Your kitten climbed up on the curio cabinet
and crashed into Mrs. Carter's coffee cup.

"Mrs. French found your frog
in her favorite feathered hat — and fainted.

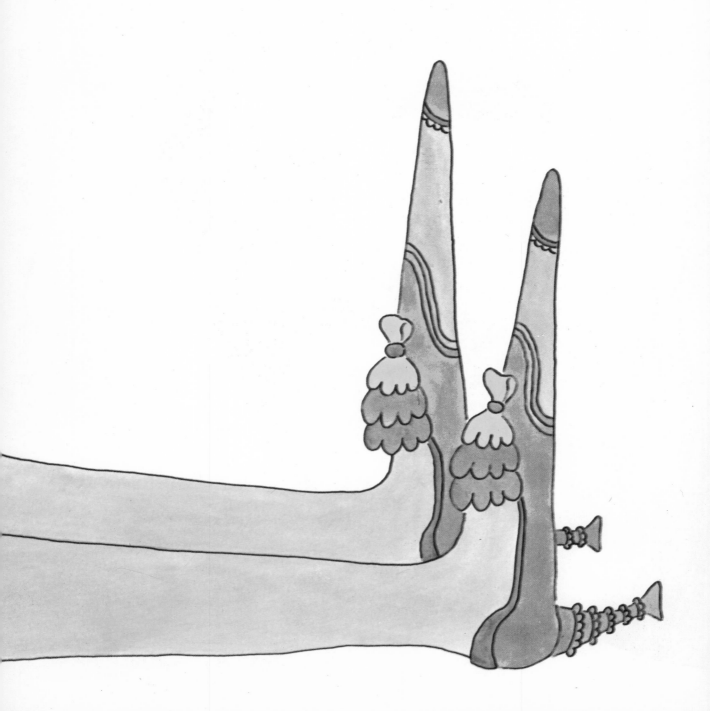

"Your dog dragged in all of Dad's dirty dungarees
and dumped them in the dining room doorway.

"Your snake scared Mrs. Smith so, that she showered shrimp salad all over our satin sofa.

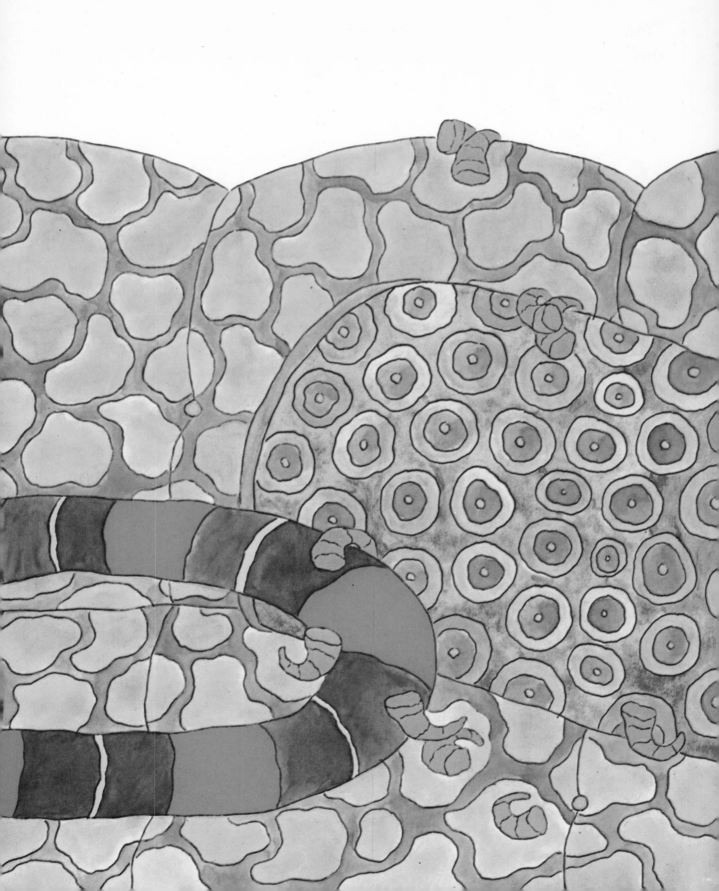

"Your hamster had her babies inside Mrs. Higgins'
hand-beaded handbag.

"Your lizard leaped on Mrs. Lester's leg,
and her lunch landed in her lap.

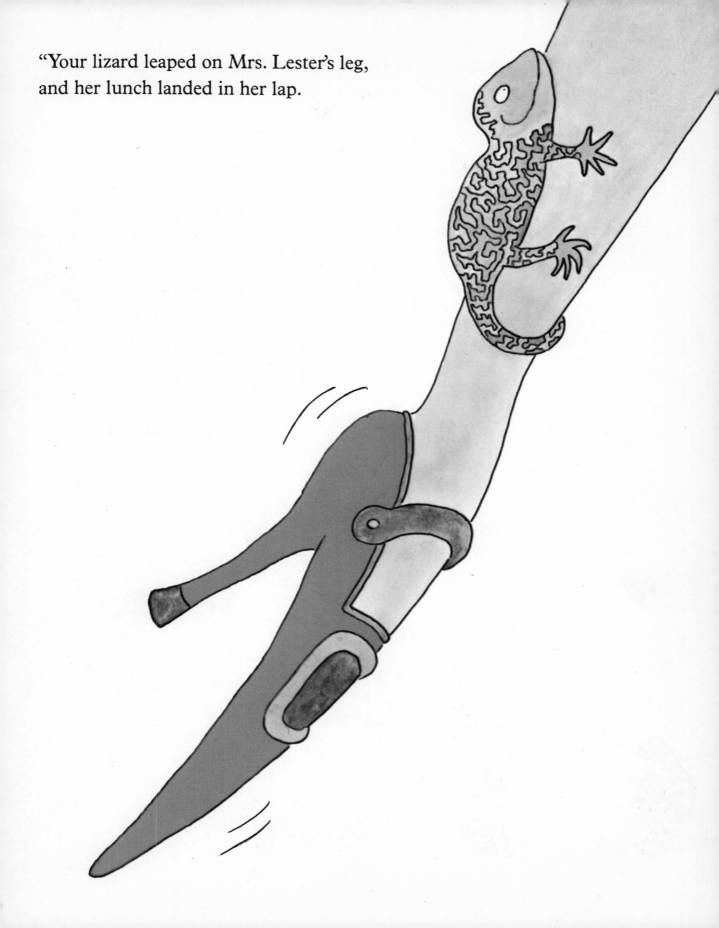

"The fishbowl fell over, and your fantails
flopped into Mrs. Franklin's fruit punch.

"Your rabbits ran right
through the room
and ruined Mrs. Richard's report
on *Restful Reading*.

"Your parrot screamed, 'PIPE DOWN, PEST!'
all during poor Mrs. Pepper's poetry.

"Your chickens chased our charming Clean-Books-for-Children chairman around the chinaberry tree."

Mother leaned back and gave another sigh. "I don't think
the Ladies Literary League will ever feel brave enough
to have lunch at our house again."
"I'm so sorry, Mom. Listen, I'll clean up. I'll do anything!"
"All right, Matthew. But first, please put your pets
in a safe place. Once is enough."
Matthew collected his pets and started to leave.

Mother stopped him. "Wait, Matthew. What was it you wanted to ask me when you first came home?"
"Never mind, Mom…"
"Matthew," Mother insisted, "go ahead and ask. I'm not angry with you — just a little upset."
Matthew shook his head sadly.
"Oh, for heaven's sake, Matthew. Ask me!"

Matthew took a very deep breath.
"Michael Myer's mouse has had more babies.
May I have a mouse, Mom?"

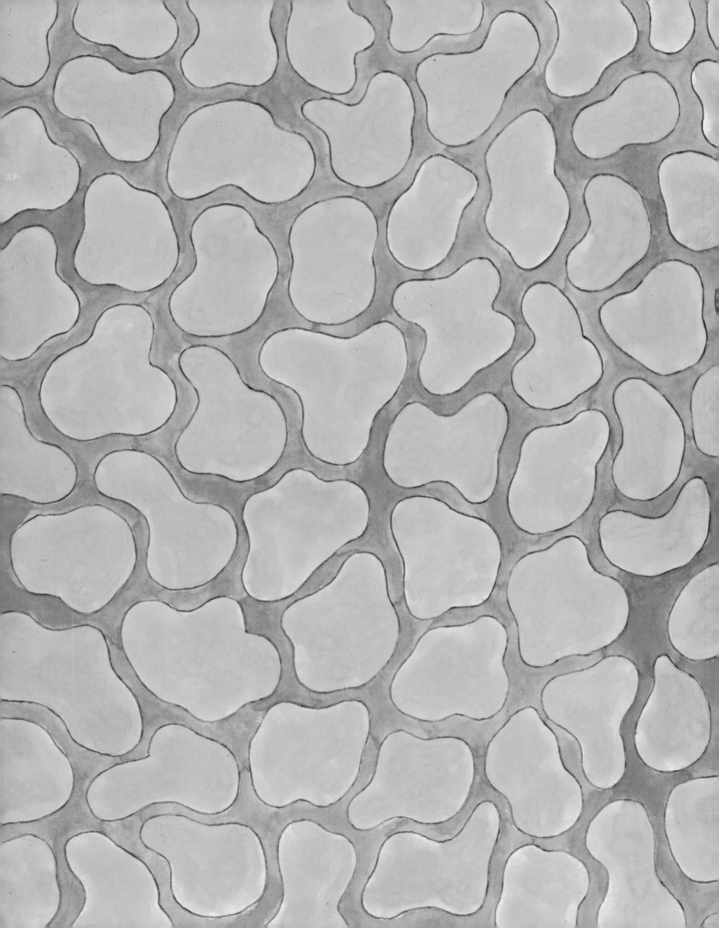